MR. SPOCK IS UNDER ATTACK!

The strange-looking creatures appear to be made of glass! You leap inside the transporter room, and it's as if you're suddenly inside a hall of mirrors. Everywhere you look, you see images of yourself and Mr. Spock.

The images are getting larger. The aliens are obviously creeping closer.

Should you start blasting with your phaser? Or should you make a run for the transporter controls and try to beam these creatures off the ship?

D0711422

If you start firing your phaser at the aliens, turn to page 53.

If you try to beam these creatures off the ship, turn to page 59.

WHICH WAY BOOKS for you to enjoy

Available from ARCHWAY paperbacks

24
WHICH WAY
BOOKS

STAR TREK:®
PHASER
FIGHT

BARBARA SIEGEL
& SCOTT SIEGEL

ILLUSTRATED BY
GORDON TOMEI

AN ARCHWAY PAPERBACK
Published by POCKET BOOKS • NEW YORK

AN ARCHWAY PAPERBACK *Original*

An Archway Paperback published by
POCKET BOOKS, a division of Simon & Schuster, Inc.
1230 Avenue of the Americas, New York, N.Y. 10020

ISBN: 0-671-63248-5

First Archway Paperback printing December, 1986

10 9 8 7 6 5 4 3 2 1

Printed in the U.S.A.

IL 3+

FOR ERIC AND CLAUDIA MINK—
THERE ARE KLINGON SHIPS AND THERE
ARE FEDERATION SHIPS, BUT THE BEST SHIP
IS FRIENDSHIP.

Attention!

Which Way Books must be read in a special way. DO NOT READ THE PAGES IN ORDER. If you do, the story will make no sense at all. Instead, follow the directions at the bottom of each page until you come to an ending. Only then should you return to the beginning and start over again, making different choices this time.

There are many possibilities for exciting adventures. Some of the endings are good; some of the endings are bad. If you meet a terrible fate, you can reverse it in your next story by making new choices.

Remember: follow the directions carefully, and have fun!

You are a young Federation ensign who has shown a great deal of promise. You have a deep interest in science and medicine, as well as a love of action. And finally you've gotten your wish—you've been beamed aboard the *Enterprise* in order to receive special training by the crew of the most famous starship in the fleet!

You're terribly excited—and nervous—as you introduce yourself to Captain Kirk, Mr. Spock, and Dr. McCoy.

Continued on page 2

The captain smiles at you, trying to put you at ease. "Starfleet Command must think a great deal of you," he says. "And I'm sure I speak for my fellow officers when I say that we're all very pleased to be part of your education."

"I just hope I don't get in anyone's way," you answer modestly.

"I'm sure you'll be a great help around here," says Dr. McCoy.

"I don't often agree with the good doctor," admits Mr. Spock, "but in this case I must concur. It is good to have you aboard."

You are enormously relieved with the warm reception you've received. But now Kirk asks which one of the three of them you want to be assigned to first.

Whom shall you choose? Will it be Captain Kirk, Mr. Spock, or Dr. McCoy?

If you choose Captain Kirk, turn to page 9.

If you choose Mr. Spock, turn to page 12.

If you choose Dr. McCoy, turn to page 16.

Dr. McCoy seems just a little too calm. If *you* had just heard the story you told, you'd want to rush right down to the transporter room right away to help Mr. Spock. No. The more you think about it, the more you're sure that Dr. McCoy didn't believe you.

And you're absolutely positive when you turn to look at him. McCoy is coming toward you with a laser needle!

The "point" is, you had better hurry and turn to page 33!

In a gasping voice, Spock begins, "The only way to defeat the aliens—"

Suddenly he lapses into a coughing fit.

"Please!" you demand. "Tell me what you know!"

When he finally catches his breath, Spock says, "Tell the captain that all he has to do is—"

Before Spock can finish, a blast from the enemy ship hits the *Enterprise*'s engine room. The starship explodes into a billion pieces!

You made the wrong choice when you decided to shoot first and ask questions later.

The End

The captain leaves the bridge with orders that he should not be disturbed. Meanwhile, you plot two different courses to the uncharted planet. The faster course would take the *Enterprise* through hostile Klingon territory. The slower course would take you perilously close to a black hole.

The decision has been left to you. Choose wisely. On which of the two courses should you steer the *Enterprise?*

If you take the course through Klingon territory, turn to page 11.

If you take the course near the black hole, turn to page 19.

You race down the hall, and the first thing you see is the ship's elevators. The doors are opening. Even before you can see who's inside, you shout, "Mr. Spock is in trouble! Quick, follow me to the transporter room!"

You race back down the hallway, believing that right behind you are members of the starship's crew.

"We'll show those creatures they can't mess with the Federation!" you declare. "Set your phasers on stun, and fire at will. Just be careful that you don't hit Mr. Spock."

As you reach the transporter room, you glance back over your shoulder to see how many allies you have.

None! The hallway is full of aliens! They were on the elevator. Which means they must be all over the ship! And now they're about to swarm all over you!

Uh-oh. Turn to page 62!

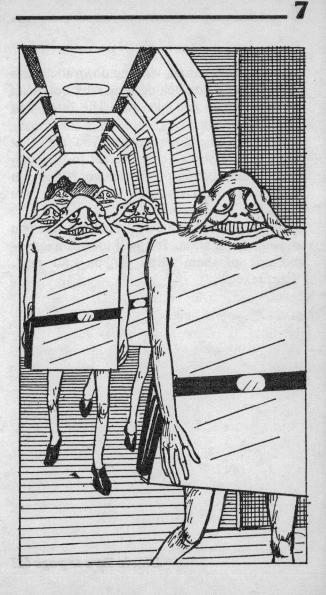

You act real casual, walking down the ship's corridors as if you belong. And why not? Half the crew looks just like you. The other half looks like Spock.

So far the aliens are ignoring you. And that ought to give you a chance to get to the communications section on the bridge. If you can just get a message through to Captain Kirk, you could save the *Enterprise!*

You step onto the elevator that will take you to your destination. It's wall-to-wall aliens— and one of them turns to you and says, "Eeezzexeq?"

Think fast and turn to page 73!

Captain Kirk leads you to the bridge of the *Enterprise*. "This is home," he says proudly, waving a hand at the nerve center of the starship. "I hope you'll like it here."

But before you can reply, Chekov, the navigator, shouts, "Meteors, Captain! Thousands of them!"

It seems as if you've entered an unknown meteor belt. Certainly there isn't anything to worry about . . . or is there?

Turn to page 15.

You watch McCoy, waiting to see if there will be any side effects. And it's a good thing you didn't give the serum to the crew, because McCoy's face suddenly changes into something indescribably horrible! His eyes become huge. In the middle of his face is a hairy ogre's nose. His mouth grows wide and his teeth become long and jagged. McCoy is a monster!

He leaps out of his bed, and with hands that look like claws, he tries to strangle you!

Hold your breath and turn to page 38.

You guide the *Enterprise* through the outer edge of the Klingon Empire, hoping to reach the uncharted planet without being spotted by your fierce enemy.

No such luck!

An entire Klingon fleet speeds to intercept you!

Turn to page 23.

Mr. Spock shows no emotion at your choice. The captain and Dr. McCoy wish you luck and hurry off to take care of their duties. Meanwhile, the Science Officer merely nods and says, "Follow me. We'll begin with a tour of the ship."

You hurry after the Vulcan—but you haven't gone far before an explosion suddenly rocks the ship, sending you and Mr. Spock flying!

Turn to page 21.

You've got all three Spocks covered with your phaser. If any of them move, you can zap them. But in the meantime you have a plan to discover if one of them is the real Spock.

Just before coming on board the *Enterprise,* you heard the funniest joke in the cosmos. You laughed for twenty minutes! Everyone at Federation Headquarters said that they'd never heard anything so hysterical in their lives.

You figure that no matter how funny that joke is, the real Spock wouldn't laugh at it. And that's your plan.

To the astonishment of the life forms staring at your deadly phaser, you smile and start to tell them a joke. . . .

To find out who the laugh will be on, turn to page 94.

The best way to save the *Enterprise* is to tell Captain Kirk in person to turn on every bit of the ship's power. So you head for the transporter room. But on your way you see two aliens (who look like you) leading Mr. Spock up the corridor.

The aliens think that you're one of them. That makes it easy for you to get behind them and knock them out.

"Come on," you shout to Mr. Spock. "Let's beam ourselves back to the *Enterprise!*"

Mr. Spock raises an eyebrow and mutters, "An ensign giving orders to a First Officer? Very interesting." Just the same, he follows after you.

Turn to page 27.

"Put up the shields," orders the captain.

"Shields up," replies Chekov.

The *Enterprise* ought to be protected now, but suddenly one of the smaller meteors crashes into the ship! Sulu, the helmsman, is rocked out of his chair. He hits his head and is knocked unconscious!

"Captain," reports Mr. Spock calmly, "my instruments report that these meteors are made of some unknown element that's capable of piercing our shields."

The captain nods, then gestures to two men from Security and says, "Get Mr. Sulu down to sickbay immediately. And you," says Kirk, pointing in your direction, "take the navigator's chair. You came aboard to get experience—well, now's your chance!"

Navigate your way to page 18.

"So, you want to see how an old country doctor does his job?" McCoy asks gruffly as he leads you to sickbay. Before you can answer, he says, "You'll find that there isn't too much to learn, because everybody on board the *Enterprise* is in peak physical condition. Frankly," he admits, "being a doctor on this ship can be awfully boring sometimes."

But when you reach sickbay, both you and Dr. McCoy—especially Dr. McCoy—are astonished to see a long line of horribly ill crew members waiting for help!

Turn to page 22.

A few seconds later, out of the darkness of space, a huge green hand surges forward at warp speed. The arm to which the hand is connected is so long that the body on the other end is in another galaxy too far away to see!

You were right! The serum you drank somehow connected your mind to the alien life form that's now attacking the ship. But is the *Enterprise*—with its quickly aging crew—strong enough to withstand this new onslaught?

With your not-so-green-hand, turn to page 32.

The meteor belt is shown on the screen. You can see the huge boulders tumbling through space toward the *Enterprise*. You hold the controls steady, watching the screen.

"Don't do anything until I give the order," says Kirk.

One of the meteors is heading right for the front of the ship. You can hardly take your eyes off of it. Why doesn't the captain say something? What's wrong? Why doesn't he give the order to evade? It's getting closer . . . closer . . . closer. If something isn't done soon, it's going to smash into the ship!

Should you continue to wait for the captain's orders? Or should you take matters into your own hands and turn the *Enterprise* away from the oncoming meteor?

If you wait for orders, turn to page 24.

If you take matters into your own hands, turn to page 34.

Not wanting to cause an intergalactic incident, you avoid Klingon territory and navigate close to the black hole.

It seems safe enough at first. But as you near the collapsed star's outer edge, its enormous gravitational force suddenly starts pulling the *Enterprise* into a web of death!

The ship begins to swirl in space like water going down a drain. If the *Enterprise* gets sucked into the black hole, you're going to be in big trouble. Or should we say small trouble? After all, the *Enterprise* will be squeezed into a size no bigger than an atom!

You're swirling faster and faster, getting closer to the ominous black hole. You've got to *do* something! But what?

Try turning to page 28.

The muscles in your face begin to twitch. Are your eyes getting larger? Is your nose getting hairy? Are your teeth becoming long and sharp?

No!

The twitch is coming from fading wrinkles, a disappearing beard—from youth returning!

The whole crew is recovering from the disease! Even Dr. McCoy is getting better. All at once a great cheer goes up throughout the *Enterprise*. In fact, it's three cheers—and they're all for you!

The End

When you regain your balance, you see Mr. Spock reading his tricorder. "Interesting," he says, raising an eyebrow.

"What is it?" you ask. "What have you found?"

"There's no time to explain," says Spock. "Call the bridge. Tell Captain Kirk that I have important information for him. Tell him that we'll meet him in the transporter room."

You hurry down the hall to the intercom system. But that's when you discover that the communication system within the ship has been knocked out!

Turn to page 26.

"It's an epidemic!" cries McCoy.

Later, as Bones conducts medical tests, you see wrinkles and beards begin to form on the faces of the sick crew members.

"Dr. McCoy!" you exclaim. "I know what's wrong!"

Bones turns around and you see that he suddenly looks older, too.

"Everyone is aging at an incredible speed!" you declare. "Including you!"

The ship's doctor nods grimly and then he points and says, "You've caught the disease yourself. You look twice your age. We've all got it. According to my calculations, if we don't find a cure soon, we're all going to die of old age within the next two hours!"

Only two hours? You'd better read fast! Hurry to page 31.

The alarm sounds throughout the ship, warning the crew to man their battle stations.

Captain Kirk is rushing back to the bridge. But before he gets there, the Klingons attack!

The blasts will strike the ship in less than one second. You have time to hit just a single button on the control panel in front of you. Should you hit the button that will put up the ship's protective shields? Or should you hit the automatic evasive action button? Whatever you're going to do, do it now!

If you put up the ship's shields, turn to page 36.

If you send the ship into evasive action, turn to page 42.

"Mr. Chekov," orders the captain, "prepare to fire a photon torpedo." To you, Kirk says, "As soon as I give Mr. Chekov the command to fire, give me Warp 12 speed. Understand?"

"But the ship might break apart at Warp 12!" you nervously reply.

"Are you questioning my orders, Ensign?"

"No, sir," you quickly answer.

You watch the meteor get incredibly close to the *Enterprise*.

"Not yet," says Kirk softly, as everyone on the bridge holds their breath.

"Not yet," repeats the captain, as the meteor looms ever closer to the ship.

Then, at the last possible second, he finally shouts, "FIRE!"

In the instant that the photon torpedo leaves the *Enterprise*, you push the ship into Warp 12 speed!

The *Enterprise* starts to rattle and shake!

Turn to page 58.

When you tell Mr. Spock that you can't reach the bridge, he immediately starts running toward the transporter room.

"What's going on?" you call out to the Vulcan, as you race to catch up to him.

"A logical question," he replies over his shoulder. "According to my readings, there's an invisible ship out there."

"You mean we're under attack?"

"Possibly," says the Science Officer, "but my readings aren't exact. I could be picking up an illusion. If that ship exists, though, one of us must beam aboard it and try to communicate with their crew."

"But if your readings are wrong and one of us beams outside the *Enterprise*—"

"—it will mean instant death," he says, finishing your thought.

When you finally reach the transporter room, you must make a life or death decision. Should you volunteer to beam outside the ship, or should you let the more experienced Spock do the job while you man the transporter controls?

If you volunteer to beam outside the ship, turn to page 30.

If you think it's wiser for Spock to beam outside, turn to page 37.

When you reach the transporter room, you see two technicians beam four Mr. Spock look-alikes off the alien ship.

"They're sending out boarding parties!"

"Obviously," agrees the Vulcan. "And just as obviously, we've got to stop them."

"Right!" You slam into one of the two transporter technicians, tackling him to the floor. Mr. Spock, however, merely places his hand on a nerve at the base of the other technician's neck and squeezes. The alien instantly collapses. So far, so good. Now hurry and get back to the *Enterprise!*

Turn to page 56.

If you hit Warp 10, and speed directly into the center of the black hole, you might be able to soar through the hole so fast that you won't get crushed. Some experts have said that it's the only way to come out the other end safely. The problem is, nobody has ever done it.

Your other choice is to use your tractor beam like a lifesaver. By attaching the beam to the nearby mystery planet, you might be able to "haul" the ship out of trouble.

But if you don't act now, you'll never get another chance. Which will it be? Soaring directly into and—hopefully—through the black hole, or using the tractor beam? The fate of the *Enterprise* is in your hands.

If you speed toward the center of the black hole, turn to page 43.

If you choose to use the tractor beam, turn to page 47.

With a lightning motion, you sweep the apple up off the food tray and, before Dr. McCoy can rip your throat open, you jam the apple up into his gaping mouth.

His pointed teeth snap down on the ripe fruit. He swallows half of the apple and spits out the rest. Then he comes after you again!

You pull away—or at least you try to. But he's got you trapped in the corner of the cubicle. You close your eyes . . .

Turn to page 83.

"Mr. Spock," you call out. "The *Enterprise* needs you! I'm just an ensign. Let me be the one who gets beamed outside."

"I can't let you do that," says Spock. "You're my responsibility."

"But it's more *logical* for me to go," you reply with a sly smile. "After all, I'm here to learn. And the best way to learn isn't by watching, it's by doing, right?"

"I can't fault your reasoning," he says reluctantly. "All right. Get up on the transporter."

You do as Spock orders. And then you watch him hit the controls . . .

Beam yourself over to page 45!

Dr. McCoy runs blood samples from the aging crew through the ship's computer. "According to my readout," he announces, "I think I can make a serum!" But after he fixes up a test tube full of a dark, bubbling liquid, he thinks he might have left out an important ingredient.

Time is running short. The crew is now twenty years older than they were just an hour ago!

You've got to make a decision. For the sake of speed, should you volunteer to test the serum on yourself? The result could be fatal! Or should you take the more cautious route and recommend that Bones try making another batch (and hope that it won't take too long)?

If you test the serum on yourself, turn to page 51.

If you think Bones should try to make a new serum, turn to page 57.

Thanks to your warning, the shields stop the monstrous green hand from crushing the *Enterprise*.

But then, in your brain, you hear the deafening rattle of the alien's voice.

"Only I can defeat this disease," says the alien. "My species has a lifetime of five hundred million of your years. Though I am dying just like you, I will last long enough to destroy every last microbe of this horrible sickness." Then, sadly, the alien adds, "I am sorry, but because the disease festers in your bodies, *you* and your kind must also be destroyed along with it!"

If you thought you were in trouble before, it's nothing compared to the mess you're in now!

Turn to page 52 (and good luck!).

Just as he's about to stick you, the *Enterprise* reels from another explosion! McCoy staggers. You try to get away from him, but he grabs you, struggling to get the sharp point of the needle near your skin. It doesn't matter where he touches you with it, because the laser needle is so strong it can even put a Klingon Flame Creature to sleep.

"I'm not crazy!" you shout at him.

"I'm just trying to help you." McCoy insists.

But that's not the kind of help you need.

Using every bit of strength you can muster, you twist the needle back against him. The pointed tip grazes his wrist—and Dr. McCoy ends up sedating himself!

As the well-meaning doctor slumps to the floor in a deep sleep, you hurry out of sickbay. You've got to find Mr. Spock!

Turn to page 50.

"The meteor's going to hit us!" you cry. "I'm turning the ship hard to starboard!"

"No!" shouts Kirk.

You ignore him and turn the *Enterprise* away from the oncoming meteor.

Unfortunately, your maneuver brought the ship directly into the path of another meteor the size of a small planet. And now there's no escape at all. You collide head on with the gigantic meteor and the *Enterprise* is turned into cosmic dust!

After less than an hour aboard ship, you directly defied the orders of the captain. Close the book and head back to Starfleet Academy for more training—especially in the area of discipline!

The End

While you try to think of a way to escape, Spock returns, getting tossed into the cell.

"Boy, am I glad you're back," you sigh with relief.

The Vulcan gives you a big smile. "I wouldn't let you down," he says, patting you on the back. "You're my friend."

Whoa! you say to yourself. This can't be Mr. Spock. This fake has shown more emotions in five seconds than the real Vulcan has shown in his entire life!

But two can play this game. And if you play it right, you just might escape. . . .

Trying not to let on that you've seen through the imposter, you suddenly clutch at your stomach and cry, "Spock, help me! The pain!"

Will you fool him?

Turn to page 49.

The Klingon blasts bounce off the energy shields around the ship.

Just then, Captain Kirk strides back up onto the bridge and asks for a status report.

"Shields are holding," you reply.

"So far," says Kirk. "But they won't hold forever. We've got to get out of here."

"I've got an idea," you say.

The captain looks at you. "Speak up, Ensign. Don't be shy."

"Well, actually, I have two ideas," you offer. "We can either try to lose the Klingon fleet by making a run past the black hole a half parsec away. Or we can go back the way we came, leading the Klingons into that meteor belt we just escaped from."

Both are bold plans. The captain, impressed, smiles at you and says, "Tell me, Ensign, which one of your two ideas do you think has the best chance of working?"

Well?

If you choose to head toward the black hole, turn to page 40.

If you choose to head back to the meteor belt, turn to page 46.

"I'm ready," Spock announces calmly, as he stands straight and tall in the transporter machine.

"Are you sure you want to beam outside the ship?" you ask, giving the Science Officer one last chance to change his mind.

"It must be done," he replies softly. "And I'm best equipped to do it."

Spock has already set the transporter coordinates to the spot where the deck of the phantom ship should be. All you have to do is turn on the machine.

"Now," says Spock.

You grit your teeth and turn on the transporter. . . .

Is there a phantom ship out there? Or is Spock lost in space?

Find out on page 41.

You're turning blue from lack of air! You've got to save yourself, except you've become old and weak. You certainly can't wrestle McCoy to the ground. But you've got to do something!

Maybe you could pinch McCoy's ogre nose. Or maybe you can stamp down on his foot—anything to distract him and force him to let you go. But hurry and choose—because in another few seconds you're going to be dead!

If you pinch McCoy's ogre nose, turn to page 54.

If you stamp down on McCoy's foot, turn to page 117.

You pretend to sulk, wandering away from the others. But what you're really doing is following Spock's tricorder reading, searching for life forms that are somewhere nearby.

It's getting dark by the time you climb through a field of broken boulders and come upon a beautiful, green valley. You look down below.

To your amazement, you think you see a flash of light—like a signal—from the middle of a lake. A second later, you catch a fleeting glimpse of something that looks like a campfire flickering inside a cave. You've got to investigate. But where should you head first, the lake or the cave?

If you head for the lake, turn to page 93.

If you head for the cave, turn to page 96.

The captain approves your plan, and the *Enterprise* starts to make its getaway toward the black hole. But the ship reacts sluggishly. The power you're using to keep up the shields is slowing you down. In order to get more speed, you switch off the shields.

Bad move!

Just as you pull away from the Klingon fleet, they fire again. And this time, without any protection, all that's left of the *Enterprise* are little pieces of debris floating in space—things like Mr. Spock's tricorder, Captain Kirk's communicator, and a strange little book called PHASER FIGHT!

The End

Your communicator suddenly crackles with static. None of the communication devices on board ship had worked before, but now yours seems to have sprung to life.

You flip your communicator open and hear Spock's voice! He's alive! But then you hear his message: "They're taking me prisoner!" he says. "I don't have much time. This is important—"

The static becomes very heavy and the rest of Spock's words are garbled. You're not sure if he said, "Jam up the transporter!" or "Jump into the transporter!"

What should you do?

If you think you should jam up the transporter, turn to page 66.

If you think you should jump into the transporter, turn to page 77.

You might have been able to evade one enemy blast. Maybe two. But the entire firepower of a Klingon fleet? Are you kidding? The *Enterprise* twists and turns, but it's a roller-coaster ride to oblivion!

Five Klingon photon torpedoes strike the *Enterprise!* The ship loses power. Lights go off. The engines quickly whine to a stop. And so does your adventure.

The End

You hit Warp 10. The *Enterprise* is no longer swirling in a wide circle toward the black hole—it's heading straight into it!

This is as fast as the *Enterprise* is designed to go. Except the incredible gravitational force of the black hole is pulling the ship toward it even faster!

The hull is beginning to crack. You can hear it. The whole ship is beginning to quiver from the strain.

You're getting closer to the center of the black hole. But the *Enterprise* is up to Warp 16! It's rattling and shaking. Circuits are burning, and instrument panels are bursting into flame. If the ship can just hold together a few seconds longer . . .

Hurry and turn to page 64!

You leap inside the transporter room—and the light reflecting off the mirrorlike glass creatures nearly blinds you! In the far corner, Mr. Spock is shielding his eyes from the brilliant reflections. The aliens are about to pounce on him.

Before you're totally blinded, should you use your phaser to blast out all the lights in the room? Or should you set your phaser on stun and shoot directly at the aliens?

If you shoot out the lights, turn to page 53.

If you shoot at the aliens, turn to page 59.

The transporter converts your body into energy and then sends it out into space. When you reassemble into your human form again, you find yourself standing on what appears to be the bridge of the *Enterprise!*

Captain Kirk, Sulu, Chekov, and the rest of the officers on the bridge turn to stare at you. These aliens must be from some sort of mirror universe, you think to yourself.

"Listen!" you shout. "You've got to stop attacking the *Enterprise!* We mean you no harm!"

Captain Kirk shakes his head sadly. "It didn't take long for our young ensign to crack, did it? What a shame. Take him down to sickbay," he orders a security team.

The last thing you hear as you're carried off the bridge is Sulu telling Kirk, "That strange force field is still out there, Captain."

That's when you realize that you're on the *real Enterprise!* You must have bounced off the force field and reassembled on the bridge! And Captain Kirk thinks you've gone crazy!

Turn to page 60.

With the captain's blessing, you turn the *Enterprise* around and race back toward the meteor belt.

The Klingons follow after you at top speed. And they're gaining on you fast! But just as you approach the meteor belt, you suddenly veer off!

Turn to page 70.

You set the tractor beam on the uncharted planet. It works! You're no longer being pulled toward certain death. In fact, you're slowly putting some distance between the *Enterprise* and the black hole!

Just then, Captain Kirk comes back to the bridge. "I see you've got everything under control," he says, complimenting your quick thinking.

"Just doing my job," you answer modestly.

"And doing it well," says the captain. "You know," he adds thoughtfully, "I could use a good officer like you when we beam down to that mystery planet. Consider yourself assigned to the landing party, Ensign."

What an honor! Let's just hope you live long enough to enjoy it!

Turn to page 55.

The minutes tick away.

Where is Spock? you keep asking yourself.

More time drags by. No Vulcan.

Suddenly you hear the unmistakable sound of photon torpedoes being fired. First one torpedo, then another, and another. And then you hear the distant sound of an explosion!

Throughout the alien ship there is thunderous squeaking. It may not be English, but you can understand cheering in any language. They blew up the *Enterprise!*

And they blew *you* right out of this book!

The End

The fake Spock is startled and he signals the two guards. They turn off the laser and join their fellow alien to see what's wrong with you.

And that's when you leap into action!

Using your ancient kung fu moves, learned from centuries-old Chuck Norris films, you clobber your three enemies.

Okay, you're free now. But what are you going to do next? The real Mr. Spock said that there was a logical way to stop the aliens. But what is it?

Two thoughts pop into your mind. One is that the *Enterprise* needs to shut down all of its power so that the duplicators have nothing to duplicate, destroying their energy source. The second thought is just the opposite—that the *Enterprise* should use all of its power in one sudden blast in order to overload the duplicator capacity, short-circuiting the enemy.

Make a choice—and hope that it's the right one!

If you think the Enterprise *should turn off its power, turn to page 8.*

If you think the Enterprise *should use all its power, turn to page 14.*

You race back to the transporter room, hoping to find the Vulcan.

He's there, all right, but he's not alone! Mr. Spock is under attack by a horde of strange-looking creatures who appear to be made out of glass!

Should you run for help, or should you join in the battle?

If you run for help, turn to page 6.

If you join the battle, turn to page 44.

Dr. McCoy is about to take a swallow from the test tube, when you grab it out of his hand. "You're too important to risk poisoning yourself!" you exclaim. "If this formula doesn't work, you've got be alive to make another." And with that, you take a big mouthful of the bubbling dark liquid and force it down your throat!

As bad as it tastes, it makes you feel even worse! You start to sweat, your tongue swells up, you can hardly breathe—and then you suddenly collapse in a heap!

If you have the nerve, turn to page 63.

"If only we had a little more time," you think to yourself.

You're stunned when the alien says, "A voice! I haven't heard a sound since all my people died of this dread disease. I am the last one left. But who are you?"

"I am an ensign on the Starship *Enterprise*," you reply in your thoughts.

Something in Dr. McCoy's serum has given you a mental link to the alien. You've got to use your ability to communicate with this creature to save the *Enterprise* and its crew. But how?

Should you try to stall the alien long enough for Dr. McCoy to make a new serum? Or, if you don't think you can keep it at bay, should you try to trick the alien so that the *Enterprise* can make a run for it?

If you try to stall for more time, turn to page 67.

If you try to trick the alien, turn to page 76.

You aim at the ceiling. *Blam . . . blam . . . blam!* One after another, you shoot out the lights, plunging the room into total darkness.

A moment later, a security detail opens the door, flooding the room with light from the corridor. But the aliens are gone!

Mr. Spock picks himself up off the floor and says, "Mirrors only live when there is light for them to reflect." And then he adds, "And I live only because of your quick thinking."

"Then would you do me a small favor?" you ask as the security detail grabs you. "Would you tell these guys to let me go?"

The head of the security detail announces, "We're going to throw the book at you for escaping from sickbay!"

"On the contrary," says Spock, "we're going to throw a Federation Medal at him! You're looking at the hero who saved the *Enterprise!*"

The End

You squeeze McCoy's nose—and he yelps in surprise, letting go of you! You take a deep breath and then call out for help.

Aging members of an *Enterprise* security detail rush into the small cubicle and help you tie McCoy down to his bed.

Bones looks like a monster, but as you watch him lying there, you realize that he's stopped aging! The cure must be very close!

You lean near the strapped-down doctor and whisper, "What should I do?"

In a rasping, wild voice, McCoy struggles to find his sanity long enough to answer. "The formula is right!" he finally replies. "It's the dosage that's wrong!"

"Should I give the crew more or less than you took?" you ask.

McCoy can't hold onto his human side any longer. He suddenly howls with rage, trying to rip the straps that hold him down.

It's useless trying to talk to him. You must choose the right dosage yourself . . .

If you give the crew half as much as McCoy took, turn to page 102.

If you give the crew twice as much as McCoy took, turn to page 104.

When the *Enterprise* reaches the planet, you join Captain Kirk, Mr. Spock, and Dr. McCoy in the transporter room. But just as you're about to beam down, a voice is piped over the communication system.

"This is Professor Jinks," says the voice. "Who are you, and why are you orbiting my planet?"

"This is the Starship *Enterprise*," Kirk replies. "We're a bit surprised to hear from you, Professor, because we didn't pick up any life forms on your planet."

"Well, I'm very much alive," laughs Professor Jinks. "So why don't you just run along now."

Turn to page 65.

You and Mr. Spock don't waste any time. But just as the two of you are about to beam yourselves back to the *Enterprise,* a red light on the transporter begins to blink.

"What is it?" you ask the Science Officer. "What's wrong with it?"

"The transporter is designed to give a warning if one of its parts is nearing a malfunction. In other words, if we try to beam ourselves over to the *Enterprise* now, we might be committing suicide."

Should you risk using the transporter? Or should you try to find some other way of getting back to the *Enterprise?*

If you risk using the transporter, beam yourself over to page 75.

If you want to find another way back to the Enterprise, *turn to page 86.*

"Make another batch?" shouts Bones, after you make your suggestion. "Are you out of your mind? There isn't time for that. The whole ship is coming down with the disease!"

He's right. Even though Captain Kirk refuses to leave the bridge, you can hear the age in his voice when he tries to calm the crew over the communication system.

"I guess you're right," you admit, as you begin to reach for the test tube. But before you get your hands on it, Dr. McCoy picks it up first and swallows every drop of the serum!

"I'll be the guinea pig," says Bones. But before he can give you any further instructions, he suddenly passes out!

Will the serum work?

Find out on page 74.

The ship is beginning to come apart at the seams!

"Reduce speed to Warp 2!" orders the captain.

You don't need to be told twice. You carefully reduce the ship's speed—and realize that you've flown through the debris from the shattered meteor, right out into clear, wide open space. You're safe!

Except your adventure has only just begun . . .

Turn to page 69.

You fire at the glass creatures, but your blast merely reflects off their mirrorlike surface and it comes flying back at you! You crumple to the ground, stunned!

While you lie there, the strange aliens pour aboard the *Enterprise,* taking it over.

"Reflect" on that for a while—and then close the book.

The End

"What's this all about?" McCoy asks the head of the security team when they drag you into sickbay.

"Looks like the young ensign couldn't stand the strain," says the head of the team.

"Is that true?" demands the doctor.

"I can explain everything," you shout just a little bit wildly. "You've just got to believe me. The fate of the *Enterprise* may hang in the balance!"

Dr. McCoy dismisses the guards. You tell him what happened, but when you're finished he doesn't seem to buy it. "If you don't believe me, ask Mr. Spock!" you insist.

"Oh, I believe you," says McCoy, patting you on the shoulder. "You just lie still now."

Does he really mean that, or is he just humoring you so he can knock you out with a needle?

If you think Dr. McCoy believes you, turn to page 71.

If you think McCoy is just humoring you, turn to page 3.

After you're thrown into the laser prison, Spock points at the two guards who look just like him and says, "They're duplicators."

"What do you mean?" you ask in confusion.

"These aliens copy almost everything—your body, your face—but most of all, your energy. And their ship duplicates, too. Didn't you notice their bridge?"

"It was kind of familiar," you admit.

"More than familiar. It was exactly the same as the *Enterprise!* says Spock. "But more important, they're duplicating the power of the *Enterprise,* taking on its energy!"

"How can we stop them?" you ask.

"Actually, it's very simple," he begins. "Indeed, it's perfectly logical. Except first we have to escape from here—and we've got to do it right away!"

But before he can tell you his plan, Spock is suddenly taken away to be interrogated.

Should you wait until he returns before you try to get away? Or should you try to escape now on your own?

If you decide to wait for Spock, turn to page 48.

If you try to escape now, turn to page 35.

You dive into the transporter room, roll over twice, and come up on your hands and knees with your phaser pointed at an alien who has Mr. Spock by the throat.

In a voice that sounds like fingernails on a chalkboard, the alien holding Spock says, "If you shoot at us, we will kill your friend!"

"Looks like you were planning on killing him anyway," you reply.

The alien laughs. Or at least it sounds like a laugh. But out of its mouth shoots a beam of red light! You roll out of the way as the light burns the floor where you were lying. Then the other aliens open their mouths and more beams of red light flash toward you. You haven't got a chance, but you figure you'll take at least one of them with you, so you fire your phaser as you roll out of the way . . .

Keep rolling to page 89!

As you lie unconscious on the floor, your mind is filled with a vivid image. In a sky full of swirling stars, you see a huge green hand reach out to crush the *Enterprise!*

The picture you see seems remarkably real. You hear a voice in your brain saying, "The disease must be destroyed. And anyone infected by it must also die before it can spread!"

You might be having a simple nightmare, or you might be getting a glimpse into the future. What do *you* think it is?

If you think you're simply dreaming, turn to page 78.

If you think this is a glimpse into the future, turn to page 85.

The *Enterprise* is streaking toward the center of the black hole at Warp 18! Warp 19! Warp 20!

The ship enters the black hole. You've gone where no man has gone before. But it's as far as you're going to get. The theory that you can come out the other end of a black hole if you enter it fast enough is just that: a theory. The fact, however, is that the *Enterprise* is squished so small that you couldn't even find it under a microscope!

As you can imagine, it's hard to hold a book in your hands when you're that tiny. Putting it another way, the book goes on, but you don't.

The End

Kirk ignores the professor. "Request permission to beam down," says the captain.

"Well, if you must," sighs Jinks. "The planet's surface is a little tricky, so to be safe, you ought to beam down to the following coordinates: 33.51.62."

"That's solid rock," says Mr. Spock to the captain.

"I know," Kirk agrees.

"We don't have any reason to believe that Professor Jinks is lying," McCoy reminds the captain and Spock.

What do you think? Should you trust Jinks?

If you trust Jinks, turn to page 82.

If you don't trust Jinks, turn to page 87.

Almost positive that Spock said, "Jam up the transporter," you immediately begin pulling wires out of the mechanism. But it's too late. Before you can tear out the guts of the machinery, three life forms from the phantom ship beam aboard—and all three of them look exactly like Spock!

Turn to page 80.

"The only way to stop the disease is to kill the carriers," announces the alien. "It's for the good of all living creatures that I must condemn you to death."

It starts to pound on the shields of the *Enterprise*.

"Wait!" you cry. "How long have you been fighting this disease?"

The alien stops to consider. "Well, now, that's a tough one. It's been—let me see—just slightly over thirty-one million years, give or take a few dozen centuries."

"Thirty-one million years," you repeat. "And you can't give us a lousy half an hour? Now is that fair?"

"Hmmmm," ponders the alien. "I suppose you've got a point."

Turn to page 72.

Well, you're ready for *almost* anything.

Five sets of arms wrestle you to the deck. Before you can fire your phaser, it's grabbed out of your hands. You're a prisoner now, just like Spock.

But where *is* the Vulcan? You look around the bridge—and that's when you realize that everybody there looks exactly like you!

One of your doubles makes several squeaking noises—that's their language—and then you're roughly hauled to your feet. You're taken to a prison made of deadly light from a laser. Spock is waiting there. But outside the prison are two guards—and as incredible as it seems, those two jailors look exactly like Spock!

"What's going on here?" you demand.

Find out on page 61.

Where did those meteors come from? And since when can they get through a starship's shields? Something strange is going on.

"Captain," reports Chekov, in a surprised voice, "I'm picking up the presence of a planet just two parsecs away. The odd thing, sir, is that our computer records show no such planet!"

"I wouldn't be surprised if those meteors and our mystery planet have something in common," says Kirk. "Let's go check it out. Plot a course to that planet, Ensign," the captain orders you.

Plot a course to page 5.

The Klingons are surprised by your maneuver. Their fleet can't turn after you that sharply, and they sweep into the meteor belt!

You intercept one of their garbled radio transmissions:"Commander to base. We blundered into the synthetic meteor belt that we created to destroy Federation starships. The planet from which they were launched is now unprotected, and our own secret weapon is going to destroy us!"

The Klingon fleet is totally decimated. But more important, now that you know the secret behind the mystery planet, you plot a new course there and blow the Klingon base into a billion pieces!

And you? Well, you showed the Klingons that you possess the greatest secret weapon of all: brains!

The End

Thank goodness Dr. McCoy believes you. You close your eyes and sigh with relief. But then, an instant later, you feel the slight tick of a laser needle piercing your skin!

You'll never know what happens next, because you sleep right through it. Good night!

The End

You convinced the alien to give you thirty more minutes, but will you have a cure that soon? You ask Bones, who replies, "We'll try. What have we got to lose?"

It's a race against the clock—in more ways than one. But suddenly Bones, who is now roughly ninety years old, begins to lose his memory! "I've made the formula," he says helplessly, "but I can't remember if I'm supposed to heat it or cool it!"

It's up to you. Heat or cool? And there's only one minute left!

If you choose to heat the serum, turn to page 110.

If you choose to cool the serum, turn to page 118.

The alien asked you a question in its squeak language—and he's waiting for an answer.

What are you going to do?

Should you respond by making some kind of squeaking sound yourself, and hope that your answer makes sense? Or should you simply shake your head, and hope that your unspoken "no" will do the trick?

Your life depends on what you do next. Good luck!

If you reply with a squeak of your own, turn to page 84.

If you reply by shaking your head "no," turn to page 98.

You lay Dr. McCoy out in an isolation cubicle and carefully watch him, looking for any signs that the aging process has stopped. As you scratch your long beard, you think you see something!

McCoy's skin is much smoother, the gray is leaving his hair, and his body seems to be getting straighter. The serum not only stopped the disease, it seems to be reversing it!

It looks like Dr. McCoy's concoction is a huge success. It takes you no time at all to mix more of the serum. But Bones hasn't awakened yet, and that worries you. You don't know yet if the drug has any side effects.

Should you ignore your concerns and give the serum to the rest of the crew? Or should you wait a little longer, until you see if anything else happens to Dr. McCoy?

It's a tough decision. But no one else can make it except you!

If you give out the serum now, turn to page 81.

If you wait before giving out the serum, turn to page 10.

"The warning light is telling us that the transporter *might* break," you point out to Spock. "But it isn't broken yet. The odds ought to be in our favor that it'll work long enough to get us home. Besides, what other way do we have of getting back to the ship?"

"You make a logical argument," he admits. "Are you sure you aren't part Vulcan?"

The two of you prepare to beam over to the *Enterprise*. You know that you're taking a risk. But reason and logic seem to be on your side. With the red warning light flashing, you beam yourselves home . . . you hope.

Discover your fate on page 92.

"Hey, you'd better move your hand away from the ship," you tell the alien, "because we've already decided to blow ourselves up."

"A noble decision," replies the alien, pulling its hand back deep into space.

Up on the bridge, Captain Kirk sees his chance. The *Enterprise* hits Warp 10 within mere seconds. Before the alien can react, you're more than fifteen million light-years away!

And you'd better travel just as fast to page 97!

You hope that you're doing what Spock wants. If you're wrong, it could spell disaster for the *Enterprise*. With Spock reporting that he was taken prisoner, you unholster your phaser. If it's a fight that the aliens want, you're ready to give it to them!

You take a deep breath, turn on the transporter, and then stand beneath its glowing light.

Within seconds, you're beamed out of the *Enterprise* and onto the bridge of the phantom ship. You're ready for anything!

Turn to page 68.

When you wake up, Dr. McCoy (who is beginning to look like the oldest man you've ever seen) hovers over you, asking, "Do you feel any different? Did anything happen?"

You remember the image of the green hand reaching out to crush the *Enterprise,* but you're sure it was nothing more than a nightmare. After all, who would believe such a thing? If you told Dr. McCoy about it, he'd think you were crazy.

You keep silent—until all of a sudden, giant green fingers rip through the shell of the *Enterprise!* One of the fingernails just misses you! Not that it matters. The *Enterprise* is quickly crushed into a tiny ball!

You saw the future—too bad, though, that you're not going to be in it!

The End

"Don't shoot! It's me!" all three life forms cry as you raise your phaser. One—or none—of the images might actually be Spock.

You're not sure what you should do. You could set your phaser on stun and shoot all three of them right away, or you could somehow try to discover if the real Spock is among them.

If you shoot all three of them, turn to page 103.

If you try to discover which one of the three life forms is Spock, turn to page 13.

Before finally taking it yourself, you give the serum to the rest of the crew. You're relieved that not a single person on the *Enterprise* has died of old age!

Just like Dr. McCoy, the whole crew gets younger and younger. Except the anti-aging serum doesn't stop! Soon the entire crew of the *Enterprise* becomes babies. And then they—and you—disappear entirely! That's when you discover something far worse than dying . . . not living at all!

The End

"It's none of my business, sir," you pipe up, full of confidence, "but our readings were wrong when they told us that there wasn't any life on the planet. The readings are probably wrong again about those coordinates being solid rock. I'm sure that this Professor Jinks must know what he's talking about. I say we trust him."

"I appreciate your opinion, Ensign," begins Kirk in a kindly voice, "but—"

In your enthusiasm, you turn on the transporter and leap into its matter converting light, saying, "I just know there won't be any problem. In fact, I'll beam down first to prove it!"

Beam down to page 95.

Seconds pass. Nothing happens.

You open your eyes. Bones—the *human* Dr. McCoy—is standing in front of you with a smile on his face. "You found the cure!" he announces. "My formula, plus an apple, will save the *Enterprise*. You're a genius! But, tell me," he asks, "how did you know that an apple was the answer?"

"Oh," you weakly reply, "I always heard that an apple a day keeps the doctor away."

The End

You tighten the muscles in your throat and, in a high-pitched voice, you squeak, "Eee eee exeee!"

The alien who asked you the question grins, and everyone else on the elevator breaks out into squeaking laughter.

It turns out that the alien wanted to know if you had tried the Beladorian salad for lunch (it's made of fruits and vegetables grown on the Beladorian asteroids).

You replied, "Smell my breath."

You got a lucky break—the Beladorian salad is famous for its sharp odors! In other words, you just "squeaked" by.

Go on to page 90.

The image is so real, so vivid, that you fight to wake yourself up.

"What is it?" Dr. McCoy asks worriedly as you stagger off your sickbay bed.

"Danger," you mutter, positive that your nightmare is about to take place.

You call Captain Kirk on the ship's communication system. "Put up the ship's protective shields!" you insist. "Hurry!"

Dr. McCoy is flabbergasted. He thinks you've gone insane.

Meanwhile, you sound so sure of yourself that the captain gambles that you know what you're talking about.

But do you really know what you're talking about—or have you gone totally nuts?

Find out on page 17.

You reluctantly head for the door. On your way out, in frustration, you pound your fist on the transporter. "Stupid machine!" you spit angrily.

The red light goes out!

"Wait!" you cry, grabbing Spock's arm. "Look at this!"

"Interesting," says Spock. "The only thing that was broken on the transporter was the warning light itself. Your blow to the mechanism apparently fixed it."

"Then we can beam back to the *Enterprise?*" you ask.

"Exactly."

So what are you waiting for? Turn to page 101!

"I may be speaking out of line," you offer, "but this whole thing seems a little fishy to me, Captain. If you don't mind my saying so, sir, I think we ought to stick with our original landing coordinates."

"I don't mind, Ensign. In fact, I was thinking exactly the same thing," agrees Kirk.

You beam down to the planet surface, ignoring the professor's suggested landing site. Lucky for you that you do, because as soon as you beam safely to the ground, Professor Jinks comes running over and, with a great deal of embarrassment, says, "Thank goodness you're all right. I'm awfully sorry about those 'underground' coordinates I gave you. The fact is, I'm bad with numbers."

Is he also bad with the truth?

Turn to page 100.

You jam the end of the banana into McCoy's huge, gaping mouth. Ah, if only you had shoved it into his mouth sideways, instead, because this way the banana simply slides straight down his throat. He doesn't even chew it. But he sure chews on you! Yecchh!

The End

Your phaser blast is high. It accidentally hits the ship's fire alarm system, causing bells to clang loudly all over the *Enterprise*. But the thunderous noise, however, literally shatters the enemy! Thin, glasslike crystals lie everywhere. But Spock is all right! And so are you!

"What did I do?" you ask in confusion.

"You saved my life," he replies. "You see," he explains, "the aliens are like mirrors. They reflect not only light, but energy. If you had fired right at them, the blast would have bounced right back at you! But because you missed, we have discovered the enemy's weakness: sound! And that's what we must tell the captain!"

Head for the bridge, via page 99.

The elevator doors finally open—and not a second too soon. Another one of the aliens had just begun talking to you. But you quickly wave and step out onto the bridge as the doors close behind you. Safe. At least for now.

Just off to your right is the communications area. You casually wander off in that direction while the alien crew continues to busily multiply its power. They ignore you.

Soon you're standing directly behind the communications officer. It's now or never . . .

You shove the alien off his chair and grab the microphone. With a quick flick of your wrist, you open all hailing frequencies. "Captain Kirk!" you cry. "You can defeat the aliens by turning off all your power! They're duplicating your energy and soon they'll be strong enough to defeat you! You've got to turn off everything! Hurry!"

You begin to repeat the message, but a blast from an alien's phaser hits the communications board and blows it up. You're thrown to the floor by the blast. And when you look up, you see every alien on the bridge pointing a phaser at you. You're going to die!

Be brave and turn to page 105.

The transporter works long enough to convert your bodies into energy—

And it continues to work long enough to send that energy out into space—

But then the transporter stops dead! And speaking of dead . . .

Your bodies never re-form—you and Mr. Spock forever blow through the galaxies on cosmic winds.

The End

You climb down into the valley and hike over to the lake. The water lapping up onto the shore is a familiar and reassuring sound—it's almost like being back on earth.

You take off your shoes and socks, roll up your uniform pant legs, and wade into the water. If someone—or something—is out there, then Professor Jinks is lying. And if he's lying, you've got to find out why!

The water feels good. You wade in a little deeper—and that's when something grabs you around the ankles!

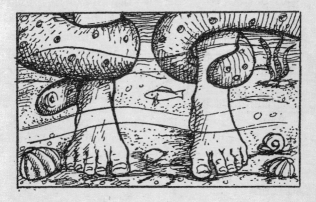

Turn to page 106.

"Hey," you begin, "why did the Zotropian cross the universe?"

In one voice, the three Spocks say, "I don't know. Why?"

"To get to the other side!" you roar, unable to keep a straight face.

Two of the Spocks break up into riotous laughter. The third one just looks at you quizzically. You're still giggling, but you manage to point your phaser at the two laughing Spocks and fire, knocking them out.

The real Mr. Spock hurries to join you at the transporter. While the two of you finish ripping it apart, the Vulcan explains, "The alien attack was only meant to distract everyone. The enemy planned to beam landing parties aboard through our transporter system and take over the *Enterprise*. But, thanks to you, their plan has been foiled."

Spock pulls the last wire out of the transporter. He turns to look at you and says, "Now that the threat is over, would you please explain to me why a Zotropian crossing the universe is so funny?"

The End

You beam down to the surface of the planet. Or, more accurately, *into* the surface of the planet!

You beamed down into solid rock! The only part of you that's visible above the rock is your hair!

Well, hair today, gone tomorrow!

The End

There's a cave dug deep into the side of the valley wall. You sneak up toward it and peer inside: you're shocked by the sight of an old man who's all tied up, surrounded by three Klingon guards!

That old man needs your help. You pull out your phaser and leap into the cave. There isn't a Klingon alive who can stop you when you're angry—and treating an old man like that really riles you up.

"In the name of the Federation," you cry, "drop your weapons!"

The Klingons scramble to their feet. But not to give up. In the Klingon language there is no word for "surrender." They're going to fight to the death—yours, they hope!

Fight for your life on page 112!

While you made your getaway, Dr. McCoy (who is now a doddering old man) has created a new serum. If this doesn't work, the whole crew will certainly die. As it is, not a single person on the *Enterprise*—including yourself—is less than sixty-five years old.

The serum is passed among the crew.

But while you wait for it to work, the huge green hand comes racing back into view! The alien has found you! There will be no tricking it this time!

Your fate awaits you on page 113.

You try to control your trembling. The last thing you want to do is look scared. Then you look at the alien who asked the question and you shake your head.

He gives a squeak of satisfaction and casually turns to talk to one of the other aliens. You got away with it! You're home free! Or are you?

Turn to page 111.

When you reach the bridge, you hear Captain Kirk give Chekov the order, "Fire photon torpedoes number one and number two at that force field at the count of three! One . . . two . . ."

"NO!" you shout. "You'll destroy the *Enterprise!*" With that you leap on Chekov, pulling him away from the photon torpedo button.

"What's going on here?" demands Captain Kirk.

Mr. Spock quickly steps forward and explains everything. And when he's finished, the captain gratefully shakes your hand, saying, "Something tells me you'd make an awfully good starship commander." And that, you well know, is the greatest compliment of all!

The End

"What kind of a professor is bad with numbers?" you ask suspiciously.

Jinks shrugs and replies, "I'm a thinker, not a counter."

"You could have killed us—" you begin. But Captain Kirk interrupts you and asks what the professor is doing on this planet.

His answer is startling. "I *invented* this planet!" he proclaims.

Meanwhile, Spock shows you his tricorder reading. It indicates that there are other life forms nearby. When you ask the professor who else is on the planet with him, he scoffs at you, saying, "Don't be ridiculous. I'm all alone here."

We'll see about that . . .

Turn to page 108.

While you slowly reshape into human and Vulcan forms, a battle is taking place in the transporter room of the *Enterprise!*

Captain Kirk and a security detail are fighting the alien boarding party that beamed aboard the starship a few minutes earlier. And the captain and his crew are losing!

The aliens think that they're getting reinforcements from their mother ship. But they're in for a big surprise.

Hurry and turn to page 114!

After the crew drinks the smaller dose of serum, you take a swallow yourself. If they're all going to turn into monsters, you don't want to be the only human on board to see it.

Captain Kirk, Mr. Spock, Scotty, (even Bones) take their medicine—and then all four hundred crew members are suspended between life and death, between humanity and something from before the dawn of man.

Will you die of old age? Will you survive only to live like wild beasts? Or will you defeat the disease and become your youthful selves again?

The answer is on page 20.

Better safe than sorry, you say to yourself—and then you fire your phaser at all three Spocks!

Two of them instantly disappear. They were fakes, obviously meant to confuse you. But the real Spock is unconscious, lying on the floor of the transporter room.

As you try to revive him, the ship is buffeted by one explosion after another. The *Enterprise* is beginning to shake apart from the powerful attack of the unseen enemy!

Finally, Spock begins to come around. He's seen the enemy and you're sure he holds the answer to the survival of the *Enterprise*.

He opens his eyes and begins to speak . . .

Find out what Spock says on page 4.

If Dr. McCoy looks like a monster, you and the rest of the crew of the *Enterprise* look like something out of a nightmare!

Everyone's head shrinks. And your faces! A third eye grows on your forehead. Your tongue

splits and turns into two horrible tusks, while your teeth look like they could literally tear through metal.

Unfortunately, though, your mind can't tear through this book. You don't understand a word of any of this, except there's something familiar about . . .

The End

"Eexee!" (Ready!) squeaks the commanding officer.

"Exweesee!" (Aim!)

You close your eyes. It's all over.

"E—"

The final command screeches to a halt in the enemy commander's throat. When you open your eyes, you see the aliens beginning to melt, disappearing into a pool of mush!

Captain Kirk must have heard your message and shut off all power. You're safe!

You quickly find Mr. Spock, and the two of you beam back aboard the ship. The aliens, defeated, head back to their phantom universe. You've saved the *Enterprise!* Not bad for an ensign—although Spock considers it quite logical that you'll get a promotion.

The End

You're pulled right off your feet! When you fall into the lake, you cry out in surprise. With your mouth wide open, the lake water comes rushing right down your throat!

Coughing and choking, you try to free yourself from whatever is holding onto your ankles. You kick your legs, but it doesn't seem to help. Worse, though, whatever is holding onto you is dragging you into deeper water!

Frantically, you pull your phaser out of your belt, set it on stun, and fire it into the dark water near your feet.

There's a terrible roar! A second later, an animal with bright, shining eyes, that looks like a cross between an octopus and a gorilla, thrashes up out of the lake.

The beast picks you up and swings you up high over its head. You're at least fifty feet up in the air when it lets you go!

Fly to page 109!

"If you're all alone here, than you won't mind my looking around," you announce to Professor Jinks.

"How dare you doubt my word!" he sputters angrily, taking a step in your direction.

The captain steps forward, saying, "I apologize for my crew member!" Then he turns to look at you and says, "I think you ought to take a walk and cool off!"

You're surprised that Kirk is siding with Jinks. But then the captain winks at you. Now you understand. He wants you to look around without alerting the professor!

Start snooping on page 39.

You head for a splashdown in the middle of the lake. It could be worse. At least you got away from that monster.

But as you fall toward the water below, you see a dozen of the same hideous creatures standing up out of the water with their arms out, waiting to catch you! Their bright, glowing eyes blink at you like signal lights—signaling your doom!

The End

You take precious time to heat the serum before finally swallowing it.

"Your time is nearly up," booms the voice of the alien in your ear. "Prepare to die."

Suddenly, your beard disappears!

Your back straightens.

Your wrinkled face becomes smooth again.

"Wait!" you cry. "We've got the cure!"

After you make more of the serum for the crew, you help the now young Dr. McCoy to fix a batch for the alien. Once you're given the coordinates, you beam the liquid directly into the alien's stomach.

"I didn't think you could do it," admits the alien. And then the huge bony hand suddenly gets smaller before it disappears. A faint voice reaches your ears: "When I first caught the disease I was very young—and small. Now I shall be young and small once again—thanks to you!"

The End

Unfortunately, the alien asked you if you were going to the bridge. You said no. But when the elevator doors open onto the bridge and you step out, the alien who asked the question is enraged. Lying in this alien culture is the worst thing you can do. It's punishable by death!

Before you can get to the communications area, the alien follows you out onto the bridge and declares for all to hear (except you—because you don't understand him) that you're a liar!

The captain grabs you by the arm and asks you if the accusation is true. You have no idea what's going on. You shook your head no the last time, so this time you try nodding your head yes.

The result? Well, let's just say that you tried your best until the very . . .

End

These Klingons are quick! They get their weapons out and fire in the blink of an eye. But you were ready for them. You dive to the ground and shoot your phaser at the one closest to the old man. You hit the Klingon square in the chest. He crumples to the ground. It's a good thing for him that you set your phaser on stun. But the Klingons aren't so thoughtful. Their weapons are set to kill.

A blast by one of your enemies rips into the ground right at your feet, creating a six-foot-deep crater. And just as you fire your phaser, you accidentally slip down into the hole.

You're in a hole in more ways than one!

Hurry! Turn to page 116!

If it's possible, the situation has gotten even worse. It's not just *one* gigantic green hand heading straight for the *Enterprise,* it's *two!* The alien obviously means to make sure that you don't escape again.

You close your eyes. This is it. But instead of the eternal silence of death, you hear thunderous applause! The alien is clapping its hands! Why? Because it scanned the interior of the *Enterprise* and discovered that Dr. McCoy's serum has destroyed the aging disease!

"I'm glad you got away. It would have been a terrible mistake to have killed such a resourceful life form as yourselves," you hear the alien say in your mind. "And if you'd be so kind," it adds in a surprisingly gentle voice, "could you fix me a few million gallons of that serum? A body my size needs a lot of medicine."

"Sure," you reply, "but please stop applauding. I'm going deaf!"

The End

_____

You and Mr. Spock leap on the backs of the enemy soldiers.

With incredible speed, you wrestle a phaser out of one of their hands. And then, before the duplicators can react, you blast all four of the fake Spocks into unconsciousness!

"Hold your fire!" Captain Kirk shouts to his security team. "It looks like they're the real McCoy—and I don't mean 'Bones'!"

"All right, you two, report," Kirk says with obvious relief in his voice.

You step back, expecting Mr. Spock to fill the captain in. Instead, the Vulcan says, "The ensign, here, will give you all the details, Captain."

"Well, go ahead, then," Kirk orders, waiting for you to speak.

Go on to page 115.

You look at Mr. Spock—this Vulcan with whom you've shared your adventure. He nods his encouragement. You take a deep breath and tell Captain Kirk everything, finishing up with your belief that the best way to defeat the duplicators is to turn on the *Enterprise*'s powerful engines—and everything else on the ship—full blast!

Then you turn to Spock and ask, "Am I right? Is that what you would have said?"

Spock almost smiles. "You've done very well," he says, "for a human."

"That means he likes you," the captain says with a grin. You couldn't have hoped for a better friend!

The End

When you fall into the crater, your phaser fires wildly over the heads of the two remaining Klingons, hitting the roof of the cave.

"We'll bury you!" one of the Klingons says, as he begins to pull the trigger.

But they're the ones who get buried! The roof above them (where your phaser hit) caves in on top of them!

That was close!

You run over and untie the old man, who announces, "I'm the real Professor Jinks. The Klingons set someone up to impersonate me while using my planet to build synthetic meteors to destroy Federation starships!"

You quickly open your communicator and tell Captain Kirk what you learned. That does it for the Jinks imposter. He's immediately imprisoned.

The Klingon plan has been stopped in its tracks. Congratulations on your "Enterprising" victory!

The End

With all the strength you can muster, you slam your heel into McCoy's foot. With an animallike shriek, he jumps away from you, holding his aching toes.

You're free! But only for an instant. With hate in his eyes, Bones opens his gaping jaws, trying to sink his sharp teeth into your neck.

At your fingertips is a food tray. On it are two fruits from earth—an apple and a banana. If you stuff one of them in his mouth, you might stop him from biting your throat. Quick, reach out and grab one!

If you reach for the apple, turn to page 29.

If you reach for the banana, turn to page 88.

Rushing as fast as you can, you race toward the microwave freezer with the vial of serum. But you're in such a hurry that you slip, and the vial goes flying out of your hands, smashing on the floor!

The next thing that smashes is the *Enterprise!* Your time is up—in every way!

The End

About the Authors and Illustrator

BARBARA SIEGEL and SCOTT SIEGEL—a sublimely happy couple who live on planet Earth in the city of New York—have written a total of twenty-five books, two-thirds of which have been for young adults. These books are in categories as varied as fantasy, horror, sports, and adventure. Their books for adults include a celebrity biography, a trivia book, and six novels. Barbara and Scott are also the authors of a soon-to-be-published young adult series called *Firebrats*—the continuing saga of a boy and girl struggling to survive a nuclear war!

GORDON TOMEI studied at the School of Visual Arts and the Art Students League in New York City. He began his art career as a "Fine Artist," holding gallery exhibitions in the New York area. Three years ago, Mr. Tomei moved into the more exciting and interesting world of commercial illustration, which he now prefers. He recently began illustrating children's books.

144